I0521250

Storylandia

The Wapshott Journal
of Fiction

Issue 40

The Wapshott Press

Storylandia, Issue 40, The Wapshott Journal of Fiction, ISSN 1947-5349, ISBN 978-1-942007-40-1 is published at intervals by the Wapshott Press, now a 501(c)(3) nonprofit, PO Box 31513, Los Angeles, California, 90031-0513, telephone 323-201-7147. All correspondence can be sent to The Wapshott Press, PO Box 31513, LA CA 90031-0513. Visit our website at www.WapshottPress.org to learn more.

Storylandia is always seeking quality original short stories, novelettes, and novellas. Please have a look at our submission guidelines at www.Storylandia.WapshottPress.org or email the editor at editor@wapshottpress.org

Donations happily accepted at www.donate.wapshottpress.org

Cover photograph "Clouds" from www. unsplash.com/wallpapers/nature/sky

Storylandia

The Wapshott Journal of Fiction

Founded in 2009

Issue 40, Winter 2022

Edited by Ginger Mayerson

Contents

Art Deco Lung

by

Louis Gallo

The Art Deco Lung

(as compiled from the secret journals of Maxfield Parrish)

I.

Parrish lay uneasily among dozens of supine, skeletal convalescents gathered for their daily airing on the terrace of Dr. Pericles Tuth's House of Invalids. Some, like Parrish himself, looked healthy enough, though tinged with fever, while disease had devastated others beyond their own most poisoned imaginings. Indeed, at the moment, as he reposed on one of the adjustable redwood deck chairs Dr. Tuth had recently imported from Venice, Parrish noted that his light muslin smock and beloved knickerbockers seemed quite out of place among the soiled bathrobes and shawls and shroud-like gowns worn by his fellow invalids who resembled prisoners rather than patients.

Nestled high in the Adirondacks, the thirty-room stone manor had served as the palatial retreat of a minor robber barons until 1885, when one sly move of Jay Gould destroyed him over-night. To save himself from both dishonor and the claws of his creditors he felt compelled to accept Dr. Tuth's ridiculously low offer. The mansion's most impressive feature, save its remarkable lack of taste, was the breezy terrace, which extended out from the main parlor and over the edge of a rounded old mountain slope upon which it had been built. Ionic columns rising from each corner served no purpose other than to convey a sense of fashionable ruin, although Parrish appreciated how they framed the opulence of early morning sunlight— exactly as if painted into place by George Bingham!

An article by Jacob Riis in the latest *Review of Reviews* had caught his attention. But he could not concentrate for long and allowed his gaze to drift down toward the pristine waters of Saranac Lake far below in the valley. The sight eased his mind, cleansed it of nagging perplexities. Not that Parrish was an unusually glum or fretful man; it simply dawned on him with sudden, outrageous clarity where he was and why: people died here! They were dying at this very moment, hemorrhaging as they turned the knob of a door, slowly suffocating in the private desolation of their rooms, losing substance until the flesh became a flimsy film no longer capable of holding their bones intact, dying always, never a moment free of it, hanging onto life by mere threads of triumphant will. But why was *he* here? He couldn't possibly be dying, not now, not when the world had just begun to notice his work. Things were going so well he'd initially dismissed the problem in his lungs as a minor setback, nothing more; but the congested organs resisted all treatment, refused to respond to even the Olympian talents and miracle therapies of Dr. Pericles Tuth, who had cured the King of Belgium, the Latvian poet laureate, fifty-two French impressionists, and a cousin of Nicholas Romanov, Czar of all Russia. Indeed, the effluvia and froth Parrish had coughed up for months looked more fetid than ever. Dr. Tuth called it "jelly." Not a good sign.

Surrounded by the most irritable lot of human beings one could imagine, Dr. Tuth was himself a volatile yet sociable man. Industrious beyond mortal calling, he seemed to be everywhere at once. He was on the terrace chatting at high speed with anyone fool enough to listen, in his office sorting through monstrous piles of invoices, he was in the examination rooms attaching bizarre machines onto the limbs of his patients, he was in the kitchen sampling Mrs. Aubert's rice pudding, he was out scaling jagged crags that rose from the valley like material extensions of his own ego. Indeed, the small, agile doctor whose rosy winter cheeks and abstract green eyes signified Progress itself had achieved ubiquity. He kept himself busier than the noisy pistons found in those new-fangled motor cars that had begun to appear even on the dirt roads of New Hampshire, where Parrish lived. His theory that all disease originated in sluggish respiratory systems meant nothing less than that people with decent lungs need never die—not in principle anyway. "Know the ant, thou sluggard," he reminded his weary patients, whose physical decline he associated with moral turpitude. Naturally, he proved his point by walking over twelve miles a day, starting at five a.m. every morning. If ever a subject thrived to testify to the curative effects of a method it was surely the hearty, robust, indefatigable Dr. Tuth. His recent meeting with Vice-President Roosevelt on the trail made his enthusiasm all the more unbearable.

"Think of what you miss when you coop yourselves up like mother hens!" he chastised his patients, particularly the males. Lazy women were far more acceptable to Dr. Tuth than lazy men because, as he proclaimed more than once to dour assemblies of temperance leaders, "women's constitutions do not lend themselves to action. But slothful men should be sentenced to hard labor."

Parrish knew exactly when Dr. Tuth bounded into the wilderness surrounding the hospital for he too had already slipped out at that harsh hour to analyze the geometry of light as it skimmed across the lake's mirrored surface. While the doctor had little interest in art or culture or any other "creative humbug," he never discouraged Parrish from his craft. "After all," he instructed, "we measure a man's health by his ability to produce. The first thing affliction impairs is production. It doesn't matter what you produce as long as you produce."

He dismissed human "parasites" who chose not to work (it did not occur to him that some people could not *find* work) as biological mistakes. "Such people," he growled, "are human only by default— either that or mortally ill and unaware of it!" Parrish suspected that Dr. Tuth numbered artists among the world's parasites, but if so he kept quiet about it. Too many of his patients were artists. Nor had he ever apparently refused the offer of a free portrait. Amateurish sketches of the doctor at different stages of his long career hung in huge gaudy frames in nearly every room of the sanatorium. In the Sun Room he appeared as a taut, lean sinew of a man in his early twenties with beads of verdigris passing for eyes; in the parlor he'd gained a few pounds and the former hollows of his cheeks bulged with health and confidence though his eyes had already shifted out of focus; in the Electric Room he looked about forty and sound as a resinous green log, except again for the eyes, which by that point had faded into misty green smudges.

While the history of Dr. Tuth's eyes might have supplied a biographer accomplished in the mode of psychological insinuation with vital insights, Parrish saw nothing in their increasing states of irresolution beyond the mystery of the man himself. None of the portraits captured the essential Dr. Tuth because Dr. Tuth was not so much one person as a human aggregate imprisoned within a single unremarkable body. Later in the century young Norman Rockwell would paint him for a cover of *The Literary Digest*, but the journal collapsed before Dr. Tuth had a chance to make his debut upon American coffee tables. Parrish never saw Rockwell's rendition but had heard through the professional grapevine that Rockwell considered it a total loss. "The guy's not drawable," he reportedly complained, as if to suggest the impotence of art to preserve in time the reality of those things most entrenched in reality, or, as in the case of Dr. Tuth, those most convinced of their own reality. Had, say, the doctor been less stable a fact, some street corner hack might have executed a reasonable facsimile. But if realism in art does correspond directly to irreality in fact, as Rockwell's failure suggests, even the deft fingers of a Sir Joshua Reynolds could not have prevailed over the single click of a camera. The photograph had not yet acquired the status of art, however, and no one with any claim to fame would have deigned to think otherwise.

But could any mere camera capture the essence of Dr. Tuth's electrical vapors or the restorative potencies he claimed for eucalyptus, both of which he bestowed upon mankind through his cherished invention, the Volt-O-Vap? One of many such devices on the scene at the century's turn, the Volt-O-Vap cured all major diseases, including cancer and dementia. To prove to the world that he was not just another charlatan Dr. Tuth offered free treatment to one Hopeless Case per year. Rumor had it that this ploy, along with the sensational ads promoting Volt-

O-Vap running every month in the back pages of periodicals like *McClure's*, *The Munsey*, *Harper's* and *The Century*, had proved so lucrative he no longer bothered to count his money. This is not to say that recent attacks on patent medicines and medical devices and even American institutions such as the Standard Oil Company did not concern him. "Is nothing sacred?" he fumed whenever news of some new expose reached the sanitarium. His response to Ida Tarbell's grim story in *McClure's* was most uncivil, no doubt because it was written by a woman.

"What kind of female openly attacks Rockefeller?" he cried to the quartet of ghostly patients who'd happened to gather at a nearby breakfast table. "I dare say it's derangement brought on by a hypertrophied uterus. I've seen it before."

It surprised no one when he promptly mailed Miss Tarbell a package containing the Volt-O-Vap, along with an invitation to spend some time at the House of Invalids. Miss Tarbell's response, which sent him howling through the halls, was curt and unkind.

Dr. Tuth envisioned a vast conspiracy of anarchists and hired syndicate thugs who spent every waking moment planning to blow up railroad stations and banks in their feverish attempts to sabotage free enterprise. The Standard Oil mess surely meant the beginning of the end. Why they'd even managed to seduce Teddy Roosevelt with their trust-busting ideas, which was something Dr. Tuth refused to understand.

"He'll come to his senses!" the doctor would snort, dashing his newspaper to the floor, "He's got to! Roosevelt's an extremist."

For all his rancor the doctor proved he was no fool by quietly withdrawing his more sensational ads from the magazines and periodicals. Needless to say, his uneasy peace with reform did nothing to improve his relations with the U.S. Post Office which he declared satanic.

"Those idiots put the Volt-O-Vap in the same class as Lydia Pinkham's vegetable soup!"

He had good reasons for defending the Volt-O-Vap. Had it not cured the King of Belgium, the Latvian poet laureate, fifty-two French impressionists and a cousin of Nicholas Romanov, Czar of all Russia? Had not the czar kissed Dr. Tuth's hand upon the latter's recent visit to Asia?

"Here's the man who will make us immortal," Nicholas boasted to Alexandra, smiling timidly at his side.

But whatever doubts and suspicions darkened his enterprise Dr. Tuth refused to allow the so-called reformers to subdue his optimism. They might make life miserable for a while, but he foresaw a day when every home in America would have a Volt-O-Vap tucked away in its medicine cabinet. "The only cause of death will be accidents!" he proclaimed.

The device came in two versions, a simple home model Dr. Tuth peddled through the mail, and the more elaborate version he used at the House of Invalids. The pie-sized copper disc could be easily affixed to a patient's chest by buttoning two leather straps attached to its sides. A flexible copper tube issuing from the center of the disc dropped into a bowl of saline and tincture of eucalyptus solution, where it then fastened to an immersed Galvano-Faradic cell. Current passed through the highly resistant filament coil between its poles and heated the solution, charging it with what Dr. Tuth called "eucalypto-static." Its vapors traveled up the tube in capillary fashion, permeated the copper disc and finally penetrated deeply into the lungs.

Patients were required to sit erectly in a chair and respire arduously for three fifteen-minute sessions a day in order to absorb enough eucalypto-static to cure scrofula, a term Dr. Tuth favored over the more sinister "tuberculosis." He thought that if a patient believed he had tuberculosis he was doomed, whereas if he believed he had scrofula anything was possible.

As Parrish stared into the lambent waters of Saranac Lake a strange foreboding came over him. He remembered reading somewhere, perhaps in *The Literary Digest* or *Scientific American*, that a man named Roentgen had discovered a form of light so potent it could bore its way through solid matter. Roentgen's x-rays made it possible to see through a human skull! The idea troubled Parrish. He had always regarded himself as an explorer of surface qualities, which, in their own way, revealed much about inner being. But suppose someone down in Menlo Park got hold of the x-ray mechanism and applied it to the graphic arts? Edison could do anything, couldn't he?

Photography had already captured the public's fancy and put a good number of illustrators out of work. The success of Frank Leslie's publications, all profusely gorged with photographs, was not exactly encouraging. Surely no one able to peer into the center of a stone or into another human being's body would go on spending money on simple drawings. Parisian bohemians would flood the market with x-ray posters. The wilder ones were probably on the verge of concocting x-ray paint at that very moment! Parrish anticipated the day when young men would send their sweethearts valentines depicting their own hearts, and every living room in the country would be decorated not with family portraits and neat little tintypes encased in gutta percha but family x-rays. (Of course, the medical prospects delighted Dr. Tuth, who had promptly ordered one of the new machines from Europe. He could not wait to pinpoint the exact location of inner tubercles. Not a day would pass before the arrival of the machine without his subjecting both patients and staff to at least one impatient outburst over the delay.)

Parrish's professional anxieties did not go unnoticed, however guardedly he covered himself. Those who knew him at this time might have aptly described him as modest, gentle but nevertheless ill at ease. More astute observers would have noticed hairlines in his public facade as worrisome as cracks in an old oil painting. Minor social transactions taxed him, people were always appearing at the wrong time; they devoured his freedom and time; they demanded his attention and freely gave him their own; they could never get enough of him. "Notice us, notice us," they seemed to plead. All Parrish wanted was to be left alone so that he could get on with rendering the serene wild beauty of a country he loved. He had made a pact with the hellish demands of his muse, although he could think of a hundred things he'd rather do than paint pictures.

To assure himself an ample degree of privacy he had built a house and studio not far from the Vermont state line near a secluded artists' colony at Cornish. There, in a region inaccessible to traffic during the long dim winter months, he taught himself the secret of iridescence. He alternated layers of transparent glaze with layers of single colors on his canvases and duplicated a luminosity found otherwise only in nature. It was tedious and exacting work; he went to bed exhausted and drained every night. But, like

Edison, he had created light.

Well aware of the risks to both soul and body, Parrish accepted his laborious self-exile as the price one had to pay when intoxicated with an obsession. His patient wife endured the virtual defection of her husband by developing interests of her own that carried her far away from New England's cruel winters to a place called Bloody Marsh. Although he never fully understood Lydia's determination to preserve Negro folkways on an island swamp off the coast of Georgia, he relished the time alone and did not encourage her to hole up with a man who was, in effect, not there. If she wanted to spend her time with darkies, well, that was her business. Nothing was less ambiguous to Parrish than individual obsession— with darkies, locomotives, sunset, whatever. All obsessions followed the same general principles and gave life meaning, however mush they subsumed the mind, devoured time and energy, always lusted for more, were impossible to sate. The alternative, zooming through history without leaving so much as a footprint behind, was unthinkable. Thus his hunger for time; he could never get enough of it. The future would not annihilate every trace of him, he would see to it. His health had obviously broken under the strain.

The Parrishes' peculiar marital arrangement did not go unobserved by those custodians of propriety who make it their life's business to censure even the slightest deviations from decorum and virtue. There was talk. Parrish received an unkind letter addressed to "Mr. Beardsley." Some aesthete! His sole motive was to make a decent enough living so he could forget about commercial assignments altogether. If, however, the climate of the times required that he feel guilty, he proved himself penitent enough by atoning for his sins and at the same time placating Lydia, whom he assumed needed placating—which was, in fact, not the case. He accomplished this by hosting an elaborate fete every summer. All the Cornish group, friends and acquaintances from New York and Washington arrived punctually by motor car, horse, carriage and train. They amused each other with original masques, applauded Ethel Barrymore's soliloquies from Shakespeare, nodded appreciatively when E. A. Robinson read a new dour poem. Walter Lippmann and Felix Frankfurter argued tirelessly over Dreyfus. Saint-Gaudens came, so did Maxwell Perkins, who said all he wanted out of life was to become a great editor. Hamlin Garland drove up in a new Locomobile. Judge Hand and William Vaughan Moody made the rounds. The image Parrish cultivated at these gatherings (as both artist and businessman he acknowledged the power of images) was that of the Serious but Affable Young Man, who, while keeping his distance, always remembered to nod his cap and mutter something about the absurd number of bicycles on the streets, the crisis in China or some such trifle.

One summer the group enticed him to play Caliban in a masque Lydia and Ethel had spent weeks preparing and for which he had provided exotic backdrops and screens. He found the role preposterous. To hunch over and grunt like an orangutan before an audience of civilized guests humiliated him to the core and drove him more deeply into exile within himself than ever. He felt greater empathy with Ariel, played by Woodrow Wilson. When they'd all gone the Serious but Affable Young Man found himself sitting alone on a boulder in the middle of a field miles from home; he found peace as he counted every star in the black sky.

Oddly enough, he found that isolation could be made bearable by writing. Painting only accentuated it. And so he wrote—in journals, dozens of them. No one knew about the journals, of course, not even Lydia, and he had no intention of ever revealing their existence, for within he recorded not only his triumphs but also his failings and deepest fears. He also recorded the ideas of other writers who interested him, toiled, for instance, with long tedious translations of a Frenchman named Bergson and the German Nietzsche, who had recently died a mindless lunatic. He studied his own copious references to Darwin and Marx only to conclude that two of the world's greatest thinkers contradicted each other. Marx seemed to say that society makes us what we are whereas Darwin held genetic forces responsible ultimately. Who was right? And what he understood about a new statistical interpretation of the Second Law of Thermodynamics, as worked out by one Ludwig Boltzmann, made life meaningless. According to Boltzmann individual events were accidents—if, indeed, they could be said to occur at all. Reality could be reduced to random sub-atomic motions conforming to the cold and sterile laws of probability.

More recently a Professor Planck had assailed reality from another angle. Planck claimed reality was discontinuous, that electrons leaped across empty space, appearing magically in one spot, then another. Nothing accounted for the way atoms moved. There were no laws except for the aggregate. Parrish hardly understood the philosophic implications of statistics well enough to grasp that Planck and Boltzmann had, within their respective disciplines, shattered classical mechanics for good, but he did sense that leaping electrons insulted the serene wisdom of J. J. Thompson, who had compared electronic orbits around a nucleus with planetary motions around the sun. He had always marveled at the dignity of Thompson's atom, but this notion of quanta, well... it defied both reason and aesthetics. Who could consceive of much less paint a random leap?

If Parrish toyed with the wilder ideas of his day in the privacy of his studio as others tinkered with Hertzian waves and homebrew magnetos, no harm there. His flirtation meant neither profound disenchantment with the world of things, admittedly a world in decay sodden with ever increasing entropy, nor inconsolable mental turmoil; he found ideas irritating and provocative rather than menacing, however shattering their content. Moreover, he had grown increasingly impatient with their extreme purity of being. Their power could not be denied, for the more he dwelled upon them, the more they seemed to cancel out parts of him. At odd moments he half seriously feared that he could come to terms with modern thought only at the expense of vanishing entirely. Yet, science, which he regarded as the most intriguing branch of modern thought, had come to be encoded in a most alien language that he could never hope to decipher. This alone kept a good portion of Parrish as earthbound as, say, Dr. Tuth. While his abject surrender before equations of the lowliest order did not exactly curb his appetite for the principles embedded deeply within those equations, it certainly convinced him that any attempt to translate them into everyday language was doomed from the start. Thus he felt chained to a reality scientists dismissed as not only impoverished but false. Words and pictures: baubles of primitive minds.

Not long before his arrival at the House of

Invalids Parrish had sealed himself in his study with a batch of scientific papers by James Joule and Clerk Maxwell. He was determined to unlock the secret of the equations once and for all. Twenty-four hours later he emerged, dizzy and glassy-eyed, feeling like a fool. His mind functioned like a defective capillary tube in one of Dr. Tuth's Volt-O-Vaps; ideas raced up to a certain point then refused to rise any further, having reached a dead-end plateau in his brain. Mathematics had the power to kill people.

Once he came upon an article lauding Harvard's Willard Gibbs as the most original mind America had ever produced. It so happened that Gibbs was working out a statistical theory of thermodynamics. Parrish could not resist. He dashed off a note to a friend at Harvard and secured copies of the mathematician's paper, hoping he had written it with laymen in mind. He took one look at the amoebic figures squirming in the text and threw it into his kiln along with Joule and Maxwell. He watched them burn to powder. Thermodynamics.

All along the artist in Parrish, prompt to give science its due, had gone on painting only things that made sense to him. He shrewdly rejected scientific illustration as a career option and dared not turn to science as a source for ideas or designs as Escher would later do. He had no desire to publicize his ignorance. It was far safer to stick with fairy tales or folklore or scenic views than to enter the fantastic realms of sub-atomic reactions and electromagnetic fields. He could paint the man-in-the-moon but not Planck's quanta or Maxwell's Demon. And what did it matter? Posters, magazine covers, advertisements for products like Royal Baking Powder and Djer-Kiss, calendars, frescoes, book designs—all money in the bank.

Along with the money came recognition, approval. The dragons he'd drawn for Kenneth Graham's story received so much acclaim the Emperor of Germany had ordered twelve copies for his private library. The Emperor of Germany!

Adrift in his musings, Parrish failed to notice that one of the most ravaged patients at the House of Invalids had drawn up a chair beside him. It was none other than Dr. Tuth's Hopeless Case of the Year. Parrish had seen but never spoken to him.

"Name's Cline," hacked the Hopeless Case as he extended a soft, feverish hand which the illustrator accepted and instantly regretted. He had made a point of avoiding physical contact with other patients, and they in turn ostracized him—not an uncommon turn of events in sanatoriums. But Cline seemed oblivious to the etiquette of paranoia, perhaps because he was so far gone, so hopeless he'd passed into a state of genuine innocence; he babbled on despite exhausting gasps for breath and seizures of violent coughing. He must have weighed only ninety pounds, and what little flesh he had drooped over his bones like loose fabric. His face was the color of slate. He looked as if he might fall over dead at any moment, which, oddly enough, did not stop him from greedily devouring the fresh banana he held in his hand.

"Dr. Tuth says bananas are the only complete food except milk. Can't stand milk, makes me puke. You like milk?"

Parrish shifted to the farther side of his chair.

"Uh, well... yes, I like milk."

Cline seemed deeply wounded. "Yeah? You're lucky then, me, I won't touch the stuff."

"I thought everybody drank milk."

"No, they don't," Cline snorted and stretched. "Say, how long you been in this dump?"

"A few months."

"Yeah? I been here about three weeks. Just getting out and around though, you know, other than meals. My family had a funeral for me before I left, figured I'd be dead in a month. But I won't be."

He coughed and spat a wad of bloody phlegm onto the concrete porch.

"Bet I'm the only guy ever went to his own funeral alive."

"It sounds awful."

"Ah, just another thing. I'm hopeless, you know. Look at me, think I look hopeless?"

"Well, I—"

"Say, you paint pictures, right?"

"I'm a painter, yes."

"Me, I'm in real estate, you know. Don't know much about pictures, not the fancy kind you paint. I seen you painting out here from my window. I been thinking—know what I'd like? A big lung, I mean, a big picture of a lung. Know why?"

Parrish couldn't guess.

"Cause I'm going to whip the bastards, that's why, you wait and see. The Doc's got me on that Volt-O-Vap machine fifteen times a day since I'm hopeless, and I'm eating these here bananas. Doc's got a friend in the Fruit Company so I can get bananas anytime I want. They come all the way from South America. I'm going to whip it, you wait. Know what I'm being saved for? Coral Gables. Just remember it was Cline who told you about Coral Gables."

"Coral Gables?"

Cline roared and slapped his thigh. "*Florida,* man!"

The slap must have jarred his system because suddenly he dug his fingers into his throat as if to tear it open. His eyeballs rolled behind their sockets and he began to twitch convulsively. Parrish leapt to his feet. How did the damned banana get into *his* hand? He threw it over the balcony.

"Nurse!" he cried, "Nurse! Nurse!"

Nurse Pickens rushed out of the Sun Room where she had been watering Dr. Tuth's collection of miniature cacti as Parrish pulled the now blue Cline out of his chair and slapped him on the back.

"This man's choking to death, Nurse!"

Nurse Pickens lumbered forth, hooked her arm around Cline's waist and led him away. By the time they reached the doorway Cline's seizure had abated and he wheezed normally once again. He turned back to Parrish and winked.

"I'm going to whip the bastards," he wheezed. "You paint me that big lung."

A few moments later Nurse Brady came for Parrish.

"Time for your vapors, Mr. Parrish," she said, or rather sang.

He had fallen in love with Nurse Brady the first time he beheld the marvelous rotundities only slightly concealed beneath her crisp white uniform. A shapely blond with high cheekbones, flashy pompadour and wonderfully square teeth, she was the kind of girl Gibson and Fisher were adorning with stoles and ascots and making famous. Parrish had seen the likes of her dozens of times in the same magazines that contained his own work.

His rivals had busily shaved pounds off of their models in ways the stolid matrons of the nineteenth century could hardly be expected to approve, but at least they had had the good sense not to deprive them of ample bosoms and hips. That regrettable transformation would occur only two decades later when John Held bestowed the flapper upon America. People had complained to Parrish that his androgynous figures lacked womanly substance, but Held's cartoon women were ridiculous. Victims of tuberculosis! So Parrish would complain almost twenty-five years later, but, for the moment, if any one diversion made life bearable it was Nurse Brady's bountiful presence. He likened its mystery to that of the quadratic equation: both were off limits, inexplicable. It was, after all, the turn of the century, and authorities like Dr. Tuth could never seem to howl enough about the evil effects of prurience. Ever alert to the exigencies of health, Parrish channeled every stray desire into illustration. Later, at the same time Held streamlined the American bosom out of existence; Sigmund Freud would explain neurosis as the improper channeling of desire into realms nature had not intended it to be channeled. It would occur to Parrish that the same profound impulse connected flappers and Freudians, but the link seemed too mysterious to pursue.

He wondered instead why a girl like Nurse Brady chose to spend her time consoling those whose afflictions made them a notoriously restive lot. As it happened she had come up several years before, a patient herself. After a speedy and complete recovery Dr. Tuth had offered her the job, which she accepted more out of inertia than any selfless instinct to comfort the sick and the dying. She knew she had the right face (not to mention figure) to break into something more glamorous, like show business or a New York chorus line, but it was far easier for a simple girl like herself to stay put than lug herself around from one vaudeville troupe to another in search of fame and fortune. Her docile nature, her inclination to do absolutely nothing eased her into the established routine of the House of Invalids smoothly and without incident, despite her deadly good looks. She performed her duties competently, if not expertly, and with a radiant good will that assuaged the agonies of the dying. In that sense she was truly Dr. Tuth's greatest asset.

Nurse Brady's official responsibilities did not include her Wednesday evening concerts in the parlor although at these she exceeded herself. Appearing promptly at seven o'clock in her starched blouse, ascot and black broadcloth skirt, the under-pinning and hoop of which made her waist scandalously thin, she seemed an illustration of ideal beauty stepping straight out of the page. The entire scene was unreal, even macabre, as Dr. Tuth's haggard, pale and emaciated patients filed docilely into the parlor attired in their Sunday best, as if on their way to some fashionable derby or spectacle. The irony of it all did not escape Parrish, who always stood on the outskirts of the room beside a massive bust of George Washington which someone had propped onto much too frail a pedestal. The father of his country now presided over a spectral company of invalids being enticed to merriment by a flighty girl who could neither play well nor sing on key. Not that anyone cared, least of all Parrish, who grew vertiginous whenever the Nurse Brady squirmed on her piano stool.

She specialized in the songs of Paul Dresser then in vogue, although she could not have known that Dresser's brother Theodore (Dreiser) had recently published a salacious novel about a girl named Carrie, a girl perhaps not too unlike herself. Within minutes she had seduced her audience out of their armchairs, luring them toward the piano where they soon lost themselves in song and camaraderie. Even wretched Cline joined in when he wasn't drowning in his own blood or devouring bananas. Dr. Tuth appeared every concert for his virtuoso rendition of "On the Banks of the Wabash." The only person who never sang to Nurse Brady's sentimental ditties was the one man whose genius she so secretly, and often not so secretly, admired.

Parrish loved music second only to painting and could not imagine life without it, but what Nurse Brady produced was not music. Nor was the metallic racket that blasted out of the fine new gramophone Dr. Tuth had stationed in a corner of the parlor. Every cylinder in the doctor's collection was a march, waltz or some vapid love song; not one serious composition could be found in the building. Recently Parrish had negotiated some commissions in New Haven, and to occupy his time between appointments had sat in on a practice session of Yale's orchestral ensemble. The bizarre compositions of a man named Charles Ives intrigued him. Ives, who was present and looked about Parrish's age but at the same time much older, interpreted the American spirit in awkward dissonances rather than the usual melodic resolution of a theme. He would appropriate some sweet old folk tune solely in order to destroy it. Yet his music had a strange, eerie and not entirely unpleasant effect. For a moment Parrish considered applying Ives's method to a painting... but no, it was too eccentric. No one would pay for it.

He followed Nurse Brady through the parlor into a narrow corridor illumined by Tiffany and Pairpoint lamps, the light of which was largely absorbed by a series of somber Oriental runners. (The century was young but Dr. Tuth's fascination with the incandescent bulb had inspired him to wire every room in the mansion—at considerable personal expense.) Cumbrous Victorian sideboards and wardrobes which seemed carved into place from the petrified remnants of ancient trees helped bestow upon the House of Invalids its characteristic ancestral gloom. Nurse Brady alone remained cheerfully immune. From the beginning Parrish had sensed that she'd singled him out for special attention.

They turned into one of the rooms off the hall, a renovated bathroom which Parrish knew well and, as usual, he sat erectly on a stool and waited for her to attach the copper disc to his chest. As she fiddled with the straps a few strands of wispy golden hair unloosened themselves from her pompadour and fell across his bare shoulders. It was a moment of extraordinary tension for a man as thoroughly decorous as he was aroused. He fidgeted in the rash stirring of his manhood as she completed her task. She could have hardly remained unaware of his passion and yet she conducted herself with her usual professional detachment. She buckled the straps, slid the Volt-O-Vap between his legs, connected capillary tube to electric cell and threw an afghan across his bony shoulders to keep him warm.

"There," she sighed dreamily, "all done.'" She touched his hand. It always amazed him that other people felt so warm. He had heard somewhere that the temperature of outer space was three degrees above absolute zero when all motion ceased. And this, he remembered, is what they called 'entropy.' And yet, the touch of Nurse Brady's fingers on his wrist now, so deliciously warm and tender.

"Thanks," said Parrish, "what would I do without you?"

Her cheeks flushed. "I don't know. What would you do?"

Why had he said it? Good Lord, he was a married man and she, a mere child. But it had slipped out anyway. Surely he'd only imagined it. The words hummed in Parrish's mind like the sound of bees in a distant field. He noticed that her face had turned bright crimson as it often did in those days and she'd become awkward, careless, nervous. She did not actually trip over the Volt-O-Vap but the toe of her shoe collided with the bowl forcefully enough to spill some of its precious eucalyptol-static onto the yellowing floor, where it gathered into furious little beads.

"Oh, me," she cried, "look at this mess! Maybe it will cure this ugly floor!"

When she bent over to wipe up the puddles with a cloth towel, the married man could no longer control himself. He breathed heavily, bestially, a Caliban in worsteds. Then he touched the white nape of her elegant, long, and arched neck. Touch, a transport, a potential yearning for fulfillment, a mysterious communion at the edges, a tantalizing itch.

"You're the Gibson girl," he murmured, and feeling himself drift away into the fine, stuporous calm induced by the Volt-O-Vap's soothing vapors, he kissed the lovely lips Nurse Brady had turned toward him for precisely that purpose. He suddenly found himself inside one of his own paintings, sporting beside the sea with a glowing creature of his own creation. But when Nurse Brady suddenly wrapped her arms around him, he jolted himself back into the cold sterile reality of the cold examination room. Mortified by his indiscretion, he found himself staring blankly into the girl's bewildered and now quite swollen face. A milky shaft of sunlight broke through one of the cracks in the frosted glass window, suffusing her with an aura of lemon, of pale morning, of bananas. *Yellow,* he thought, one of the opaque colors. Then, as the lemon grew denser and richer, its hue darkened and he saw that she was a rare artifact sealed in amber. The random motion of atoms had ceased. Absolute zero or absolute rapture?

"Forgive me," he whispered, panting heavily. His heart raced, his mind short-circuited, he felt faint.

A perfect "oh" escaped the valentine of her pursed carmine lips.

II.

One morning in the spring of 1930 Maxfield Parrish emerged from his studio carrying a light valise and two large frames wrapped in brown paper. He tossed the valise, which contained a toothbrush and change of underwear, onto the back seat of his turquoise Packard and set the frames upright on the front passenger side. Then, sliding behind the wheel, he began the long drive to Saranac Lake.

His lungs had cleared up long ago, no thanks to Dr. Tuth or his absurd Volt-O-Vap. He'd recovered his health on an Arizona ranch arid as the cow skulls embedded in the sand surrounding it. He had no valid medical reason for returning to the House of Invalids now; he did not even know if the sanatorium still stood, although surely the time, effort and expense required to dismantle it would have been enormous and hardly worth the trouble. Parrish wanted to stand on the terrace and get one last look at the lake, at a certain slant of light he'd always intended to use but never had and now only vaguely remembered. *And Dr. Tuth's eyes.* At odd moments during the last thirty years their muted glow had returned to him. The color was no problem—Parrish's sensational blending of verdigris and cobalt had earned him an international reputation—their sheen, that's what he wanted. No such quality existed in nature. It was as if someone had wiped furniture wax into Dr. Tuth's eyes and buffed them to a soft satin finish.

Parrish did not ask himself whether or not he expected to find the mad old man alive. Why shouldn't he be? There were so many Dr. Tuth's to kill, surely one of them had survived. Parrish himself was now sixty-one years old and not nearly as vigorous as the amount of work he produced led people to believe. He'd seen the stolid past of his youth crumble; new ideas, institutions, new faces had displaced those he valued, those making life coherent. The great magazines were gone: *The World's Work, Century, McLure's, Scribner's, The Munsey* and numerous more. Friends had disappeared as well, reminding him that entropy's silent enterprise spared no man and no man's accomplishment. He remembered his last visit to see poor Wilson who lay paralyzed in the White House. Half the President's face seemed to have melted into his pillow. Parrish saw in his agony the dissonance he'd once heard in Ives's music; it had finally taken form and entered history as the Great War, the League failure and Teapot Dome Fiasco, economic collapse; it had put millions out of work. Some killed themselves, others became hoboes or gangsters, even communists. The mood of the country had soured. On that last visit to the dying President, Parrish listened as Wilson gurgled into his ear, "M.P., the world has turned to shit. You paint lies." A thick string of spittle inched down his chin.

Harding was also dead, by his own hand some said. And Roosevelt. The country Parrish still painted as a resplendent dream had indeed changed; Wilson was right. He'd seen automobiles and radios and airplanes and motion pictures and telephones harden people, rob them of what little pastoral innocence they had left, change the coordinates of space and time. He watched incredulously as young women extricated themselves from husbands, lovers and the bondage of their mothers in order to seize control of the nation's typewriters. They smoked, they cursed, they exposed themselves in speakeasies. They all looked like Zelda Fitzgerald. Even the Gibson Girl was dead.

Yet for all this Parrish had little cause to complain. He was rich and famous, the most famous artist in America, and by 1930 he presided majestically over that fame as does a potentate over his harem. His "blue" pictures had thrilled and to some extent created the Roaring Twenties. They hung in libraries, in bus stations and hotels and theaters, in college dorms, in restaurants; they graced the mantles of Park Avenue as well as the weatherboard walls of Hooverville. One could say they helped glue together fragments of a country that had begun to rip apart at its seams. In their way they were art's answer to Planck's discontinuity.

Parrish's only true competition in the profession was the young, meteoric Rockwell, who was living down in New Rochelle, where, it seemed, *everyone* lived. Flagg, Christy, Gibson, Joe Leyendecker, Rockwell—they all lived in the same neighborhood! Parrish thought that Coles Phillips, who'd died three years earlier, was the best of the lot. Phillips had done more for Holeproof Hosiery, and therefore American business, than the leagues of "scientific managers" who were claiming they had demystified capitalism. He detected in Phillips' work an unearthly quality and color scheme not dissimilar to his own, whereas he looked upon Rockwell's Boy Scout realism with lofty disdain. No doubt, though, the man was fast ascending to his star; his legendary trip to see George Lorimer of *The Saturday Evening Post* inspired every hungry illustrator in the country and induced spasms of envy and discontent. Rockwell just wasn't that good. Joe Leyendecker, whose ideas he *stole*, did much better work. Parrish found little to commend in Rockwell's tiresome imps and tricycles and cowardly dogs and filthy untied tennis shoes, cheerful postmen and punctual milkmen and sweethearts sharing sundaes at some blissful corner drugstore. The entire pageant of wholesome small-town rubes infuriated him. Reality was not like that so why pretend it was? Reality was far worse than a fellow like Rockwell could imagine, although he had heard rumors that Rockwell suffered enormous inner demons. In reality half the Boy Scouts of America lay dying of tuberculosis; the other half had been blown apart on the banks of the Marne. If Rockwell chose to touch up reality with rouge and lipstick as one beautifies a corpse, well... he'd have to settle the matter with his own conscience. Parrish elected to invent a new reality; indeed, that was the great appeal of his art. What bewildered him was that the same people who admired Rockwell's inane facsimiles were at the same time demanding more of *his* poetic visions. The proof lay in his pocketbook. What could it mean?

Rockwell aside, Parrish believed the greatest

threat to his hegemony, indeed, to illustration itself, lay nascent in other quarters. Whenever he'd taken a night off to visit the local nickelodeon, he'd been amazed by the new animated cartoons created out in California by a kid named Disney. A few years ago Disney's Oswald Rabbit had conquered New York. Now something called "Mickey Mouse" was conquering the country. Parrish had seen *Steamboat Willie* nine times and each time he'd left the theater in a state of excited confusion. Disney was another escapist, like himself; Parrish knew enough about cartoons and caricatures to recognize the symptoms. But his own blue pictures were not cartoons at all—they were serious denials of poverty and injustice, disease and despair and death. Rockwell merely pretended such things didn't exist. Disney didn't *know* they existed and proceeded accordingly. Disney didn't live in this world at all. His fantasies leapt off the screen an annihilated reality, like the anti-matter people were talking about. No telling what a fellow like Disney would do next. One thing was certain: he packed the theaters. The x-ray art Parrish had foreseen long ago in a moment of anxiety had never materialized, but these moving cartoons...they were here to stay.

One of his complaints about the movies, that they moved *too fast*, applied equally well to history. It seemed as if time itself had accelerated. It moved so fast the old illustrator found it more ludicrous than menacing. Judged by art alone the America of 1930 and the America of 1900 were two different countries. Illustrators had abandoned the lazy sinuosities and fantastic imagery of fin de siècle taste for the hard straight lines and geometric audacity of what came to be known as Art Deco. This transition from Art Nouveau to Deco, that is, from Beardsley and Mucha to Erte and Louis Icart, had proceeded quietly, unconsciously, for quite some time. Only artists themselves sensed it. It took approximately thirty years for Art Deco to gain official recognition at the Paris Exhibition of Decorative and industrial Arts.

That year was 1925. By then designers had changed the way the world looked. One could buy Art Deco jewelry, Art Deco furniture, Art Deco pottery and perfume bottles and water pitchers, Art Deco lamps, Art Deco buttons, figurines, cigarette cases, even Art Deco automobiles, like Parrish's Packard. It was a style of unrestrained pretense at its worst and controlled yearning at its best. It was nervy and vain, aloof, disdainful; it was pure pose. John Held's flappers and Coles Phillips' Fadeaway Girls were supremely Deco. So were Erte's covers for *Harper's Bazaa*r. So were Maxfield Parrish's blue pictures. Rudolph Valentino and Greta Garbo had Art Deco souls. Deco epitomized what happened to the world after the Great War. No longer nurturing, no longer sweetly laissez faire, it had turned into a hive of glass and steel; it had turned ironic.

Irony flourished in science as nowhere else. Only three people in the entire world understood Einstein's Theory of Relativity, man's most important intellectual advance since Newton formulated gravity. These three people were saying light was both a stream of particles and a wave. They said it bent as it shot past the sun. They said space curved and was shaped like a saddle. They said the finite but unbounded universe would expand until it collapsed. Matter, they said, could be transformed into energy and vice-versa. They said the Uncertainty Principle proved you could determine where something was or how fast it moved but not both. They said observers changed reality by looking at it. They said reality was a dream. They said reality was an illusion, that rocks and trees and buildings, even people, were composed of something called 'wave functions,' which had no solidity until those waves collapsed and transmuted into material particles.

Whatever they said was too much for Parrish, who had finally lost his patience. If the experts expected him to believe that yardsticks shrunk or elevators accelerated or clocks slowed down or that space travelers could leave the planet and return years later *before they were born!*, why then he'd be done with it; science had become perverse. Surely Euclid and Copernicus and Newton had nothing of the sort in mind. He bade his adieu gently and full of regrets, as one forsakes a favorite mistress, and turned to his easel with renewed, almost sacrificial zeal. It would never occur to him that science had directly abetted his career. Despite heroic efforts to keep science out of art, out of his art at any rate, he failed. His blue pictures were, of all things...statistical! They tapped an impulse to which Paul Revere had yielded when he printed pirated depictions of the Boston Massacre almost two centuries earlier. Illustration had been a silently statistical enterprise all along— but no one realized it. It began for Parrish back in 1916 when a candy store magnate named Clarence Crane commissioned him to design paper wrappings for his confectionery boxes. Parrish found it difficult to work with Crane because the man constantly mourned the loss of his son, Hart, who was in fact still alive. Crane considered his son worse than dead because he had chosen poetry over business, sin over common decency. Hart's life was a public scandal. Although Parrish never met the depraved poet, nor cared to, he did at Clarence's insistence read a few of his poems. He disliked them intensely. They were Art Deco poems.

For some reason Art Deco translated poorly into language. In retrospect, it rings memorably only in cinema, and, as it happened, talkies arrived just in time to distract Americans from economic malaise. They had no jobs, no food, no hope—but they had Hollywood. For a dime they could step off the hellish streets and spend an hour or two in the paradise of their choice. They packed the theaters during the Great Depression; Hollywood flourished as it never would again. In the films of the period, particularly the gangster sagas and comedies, they heard Art Deco speaking, speaking to *them*, the people. The convoluted syntax of a Hart Crane had filtered down and cleansed itself of impurity and pretense. It was living language and irony saturated it. In what other vernacular would ruthless desperadoes use the word "daffy"? Mae West and Harlow arrested conversation with salty barbs that, among other things, transformed flappers into vamps. Al Jolson was an Art Deco negro who spoke Art Deco jive. But the greatest Art Deco voice of them all was FDR's, and it commanded the radios of the land. Deco could be soothing, it could lull, it could be harsh and abrasive, it could sell cars and win hearts. The only thing it could not do was survive. As usual with such things, women saw to that. They gained weight. They became mothers and sweethearts again. Shirley Temple and the Dionne Quintuplets were just about to reintroduce innocent charm. By the onset of World War II Deco would lose its brazen edge, its nervy elan.

Parrish's dislike of Hart Crane's poetry did not extend to Art Deco in general; it had, after all, made him a fortune, however sentimentalized his rendition. He borrowed not only its style but its structural and geometric properties as well to modernize what he knew best: the dreamy idealism of art nouveau. If he lacked the strident irony of artists born a generation after him, all the better, for he was not interested in their world at all, not even enough to rebel against it. Only in his later landscapes would he approximate "reality" in a way those who believe the word means something expect it to be approximated.

Meanwhile, Parrish's candy wrappers pleased Clarence Crane immensely. He proposed a business partnership: Parrish would paint originals while he, Crane, would take care of the rest, which meant reproducing and distributing them across the country. Parrish thought it over and decided to give it a whirl. What neither man anticipated was that public demand would so quickly exceed supply. Within three years the frazzled Crane turned his interest over to an outfit called the House of Art, which, in 1923, released what immediately became the best-selling print in America, perhaps the world. It was called *Daybreak*. It was the most beloved blue picture Parrish ever painted.

The mass distribution of Parrish prints was statistical in the same way that large assemblies of particles conform to laws of probability. Individual particles conform to no laws at all. They can hardly be said to exist. Similarly, a single *Daybreak* meant nothing; it wasn't even much of a painting. But who could ignore tens of thousands of *Daybreaks*? Sales figures could be measured and analyzed and used to predict probable future distributions. Parrish and his collaborators were doing for art what Eli Whitney had done for rifles and Henry Ford for automobiles. They were not the first to statisticize art, however; Louis

Prang and Currier & Ives had produced greeting cards and wall decorations on the assembly line. But Prang and Currier & Ives were corporate entities; both firms hired hacks and dozens of lonely widows to create and hand-color the designs they sold whereas Parrish held himself responsible for his work from start to finish. Even here he followed the lead of commercial artists like Remington, Fisher and Howard Chandler Christy. Yet none of his forerunners grew into personal institutions as Parrish did in the 1920s. The idyllic musings of Maxfield Parrish became those of the nation. If this aesthetic fad provided the sprawling masses with a semblance of common purpose and spirit, it also liberated them from the curse of personal taste forever.

Parrish did not see this as the social threat he might have years earlier. Men, he reasoned, had at last ceased to be significant; statistics proved it; men were about as sovereign now as the motes dancing in a sunbeam. A mote himself, Parrish flowed with the inexorable currents of history and time, providing, as he felt he was destined to provide, the greatest good for the greatest number. Once he finished a painting he turned it over to the House of Art and no longer felt any obligation to it; a larger, impersonal destiny intervened. But as his fame spread and sales soared into the tens of thousands, the meaning of art, his life's work—and of life itself for that matter—grew more remote than ever. They connected in some minor way he could not fathom; they went on—that's about all he knew, though sometimes he doubted even that. Perhaps the nihilists were right all along: it didn't make any difference whether you emulated Jesus or shot a pistol into the crowd. Parrish was well aware that all sane theories of art were being superseded by the proclamations of hysterical Dadaists and Cubists and tireless fanatics who took upon faith whatever new absurdity issued from the pen of one Andre Breton, codifier of anarchy. One could not fight them, no, they were young, legion, relentless. But one did not have to join them! One could go on dreaming dreams and seeing visions.

Indeed, fleeting images from other times and places constantly reminded Parrish that he'd witnessed the demise of a simpler and better world. He remembered, for instance, his naive excitement at the Chicago's World Fair almost forty years before, when he was twenty-three years old. Science then seemed a reasonable if not the noblest of man's undertakings. He marveled at exhibits of technological progress with the awe of a savage who acquires a wristwatch. In the Hall of Dynamos he spotted prissy old Henry Adams taking notes and signing autographs. He pulled a crumpled receipt for linseed oil, upon which he had drawn a sketch of Old King Cole, out of his pocket. Embarrassed, he held the scrap out to the writer, who, it seemed to Parrish at the time, signed it with royal disdain. One afternoon many years later, as he settled down with *The Education*, it dawned on him that what Adams admired in the Virgin *he* had always attributed to light. Adams assumed that power had shifted to the Dynamo. Yet light transcended both Virgin and Dynamo. Whoever understood light understood everything.

III

He reached Saranac Lake at dusk and began the steep ascent up the Mountains of Sighs, as the patients used to call it. Nothing had changed! He remembered every tree, every stone, every nuance in the landscape, even the air smelled its familiar wintergreen. Soon the sanitarium itself came into view. It had shifted dangerously and looked as if it might slide down the mountain into the lake at any moment. Weeds sprang from fissures in the foundation. Huge blocks of stone had detached themselves from the structure and lay scattered like astrological relics. What overwhelmed Parrish was not the passage of so much time but his feeling that time had stopped altogether. The thirty-year interval seemed compressed into an infinitely small point in spacetime, a singularity. He had never been born; he would never die; he would forever be about to enter the House of Invalids. The mansion, protected within its resinous coat of eternity, a place where so many had died, had become a monument to permanence! And suddenly Parrish understood that his own fate and that of the building were inextricably linked.

He climbed the shattered marble steps on his way to the main entrance. A once stately door had broken free of its upper hinge and jammed in the casement; years of rain and snow had reduced the wood to fuzzy pulp. Parrish stepped over the wreck into the drafty mansion. The entrance hall was dark and cool, musty. He saw the skeleton of a rabbit crumbling on one of the faded Orientals. The old lamps, situated exactly as he remembered them, were, like everything else, encrusted with a sticky, coarse dust. One of Dr. Tuth's last portraits, now blackened with mildew, hung crookedly on a cracked, yellowed wall. Surely no one was around.

He decided to drive back to the village, rent a room and return the next morning to assay the extent of the damage in better light... but just then he heard music, the crackling, nasal honk of that old gramophone! He inched cautiously on the loose tiles, past the old examination rooms, the Sun and Electric Rooms, where he'd spent many hours absorbing eucalypto-static... he had nothing to fear... probably just some hobo... they were everywhere these days. The parlor door was slightly ajar and soft yellow light spilled from the crack.

"Hallooo," he called. *Seem friendly, not a threat.*

No response. Perhaps whoever was there had fallen asleep or was armed and lay in wait. He recognized the song–"The Outcast Unknown" by Paul Dresser, one of Nurse Brady's favorites.

"Hallooo!"

Nothing. He pushed open the door to an unfamiliar room, a lounge of sorts he only vaguely recalled, and spotted the man in a stuffed armchair stationed close to the machine. He saw only his bald dome rising above the antimacassar but recognized the phrenology instantly. Cline! A woman's legs also draped over one end of the stuffed chair; she lounged intimately, shamelessly, across Cline's lap. When she began to hum and occasionally sing along with the cylinder, Parrish recognized the sweet, dolorous and enchanting voice of Nurse Brady, rusted with age as it was. "Donnnn't," she giggled, reaching for a bottle of liquor on the floor. Bootleg, no doubt. Parrish stood transfixed as if encountering a ghastly pair of Lazaruses risen from the dead. The Gibson Girl and Hopeless Case together, here, now, wrapped in each other's slobbery arms, drunk and debauched.

When Nurse Brady rose to gather herself she saw the ashen-faced illustrator suspended in the doorway like an incredulous apparition. Her hair, now the color of aluminum, flared in every direction, in wild spikes, zigzags, flurries. Deep furrows and purplish splotches flawed her otherwise stately countenance. She wore lipstick, smudged on carelessly, some of which had rubbed off onto her front teeth. Her blouse wrinkled and unbuttoned. She stood, squat, widened, in her stockinged feet.

"Mr. Parrish!"

Cline shot out of the chair and stationed himself in front of the woman as if to shield her from attack. When he too recognized his old friend, he dropped his guard and grinned warmly.

"Well, I'll be damned. If it ain't the painter! I ain't seen you since nineteen-ought-one!"

Attired in a fluted, soiled undershirt, Cline looked better, healthier, more robust than he did thirty years earlier, if such reversal and transformation were possible. He had lost his hair, all of it, but his weight had evened out and there was color in his face. Parrish was not sure which Cline he preferred, this new paragon or the former Hopeless Case.

"Bet you're surprised to see me," he laughed.

But Parrish wasn't surprised. He had assumed all along that Cline would survive and was genuinely happy to see him now. He stepped forward into the light and shook both of their hands.

"How about Dr. Tuth?" he asked.

"The old buzzard's still kicking," said Cline, "amazing, eh? He's upstairs asleep. Sleeps most of the time now. Preparing, I guess."

Parrish stood grinning like some child learning that the candy had arrived.

"No big deal," Cline shrugged. "We just feed him bananas all the time. They saved me, didn't they? Once he went blind he sort of gave up, you know. It was that x-ray machine, ask me. It's the bananas keeping him alive. Know what's weird? He don't even like them. Me, I like whatever saves me."

Nurse Brady lighted a Lucky Strike, exhaled a perfect nebula from his lips and asked Parrish if he wanted a drink.

"No thanks," he said, avoiding her eyes. "You say Dr. Tuth is blind? X-rays?"

"You remember how he yearned for that machine. Well, it finally came, from Germany I think, in a bunch of heavy wooden crates. We all helped him put it together. Who knows if we did it right. He used to claim the x-rays leaked out and blinded him. Now he doesn't claim anything. We've still got the machine. What a contraption. Down in the basement. All broken and dusty now."

Parrish only half-listened as if his mind itself were a crossroads. "But his eyes still *look* the same, don't they?" he asked meekly.

"Yeah," Cline shrugged, "except for the cataracts. Sometimes you can't see them, in the right light. Sometimes milky and creepy. Said he didn't want no operation though, and now it's too late, he's too old. Hey, you'll see him, don't worry. Sure you don't want that drink?"

"Better not, Cline, thanks, I'm pretty tired. I thought I'd drive down to the motel–"

"Are you nuts? We got nearly thirty rooms to spare right here. Ain't had a case since '21. You just go get your grips, you're staying here tonight."

Parrish did not want to spend the night in the House of Invalids, but there was no arguing with Cline or Nurse Brady, so he fetched his satchels, valise, easel and the frames and allowed himself to be escorted to none other than his old room. Barren except for the now tarnished and slightly rusted medical bed upon which he had coughed himself to sleep many a night. Fresh sheets that smelled of lemon, sunlight and bananas. Nurse Brady spread a down comforter across the bed and patted it smooth.

"Have you been here all this time?" Parrish asked, reaching for a pillowcase.

She snatched it from his fingers. "Oh, let me do that. Yeah, here, both of us. A lot has happened."

The tone of her voice disturbed him. She seemed dreamy, sexual, yearning. He longed to be back in New Hampshire in his own bed. Why had he returned to this wretched place?

"Tell me, how many people have... died in this room?"

"Everybody who had it," she said flatly now, as if registering his extreme disinterest and playing tit for tat, "except you."

The urgent, brisk smell of frying bacon awoke him at dawn. He dressed, made the bed and carried his frames down the stairs as he made his way to the kitchen over which cranky Mrs. Aubert had once presided. The memory of her tart gooseberry pie exploded on his tongue. Nurse Brady was plucking some eggs out of a brand new electric refrigerator while Cline squeezed orange juice into a pink Art Deco pitcher. Manhattan style. Into the juice he tossed some of the banana slices piled high on a platter.

"Morning, Parrish."

"Same to you. Sure smells good in here."

"You just leave everything to us. Sit down, man, eat some food."

Parrish seated himself before a steaming plate of bacon, scrambled eggs, hominy and banana fritters. Cline poured the juice then also sat, rubbing his hands. Parrish envied his easy, uncomplicated relish for life.

"Nothing like grub to break in a new day!" Cline exclaimed. "That's what I'd hate about being dead, Parrish. What do you *eat*?" He thought the insight marvelously funny and guffawed, spraying grits across the table.

"Cline!" scolded Nurse Brady.

"Jeez, I'm sorry, hon, hey, I'd better calm down. Sorry, Parrish, did it get on you?"

"It's nothing," Parrish said, wiping his face with a starched linen napkin.

"Just like you to spit all over a guest," Nurse Brady would not let it go.

The last thing Parrish wanted to witness was a domestic squabble. "So how long have you two been married?" he asked.

Neither Cline nor Nurse Brady seemed inclined to answer the question, though finally Cline mumbled, "What, hon, been together about twenty-nine years? Can you beat that, Parrish, nearly three decades!"

Parrish smiled, shook his head in feigned amazement.

"Funny thing, nothing's changed much. Just look around. We're the only things that change, I guess."

Then Cline spotted the wrapped canvasses. "Hey, what you got there? Bet it's pictures."

He swallowed a gigantic spoonful of scrambled eggs.

"Yes, pictures... a little late maybe. They're for you."

Cline reached for one of the canvasses, tore off the wraps and held it out at arm's length, examining it carefully.

"Well, ain't that something!"

"What is it?" Nurse Brady asked.

"I think it's a lung, real strange looking lung. You did it, Parrish, you painted me a lung. How come it's blue?"

"I'll be," said Nurse Brady, leaning over Cline's shoulder to take a look.

"It's what you call an Art Deco lung. I only used straight lines and it's blue because... it's blue. Actually, quite a few shades of blue, cerulean to cobalt and everything in between."

Parrish neglected to say that some decades earlier he had received a large anonymous envelope in the mail. It contained an x-ray plate of a tubercular lung. A note attached to the film with a circular brass clip read "Now THIS is art!" Parrish gazed at the shadowy organ with horror and fascination. Bilateral pulmonary infiltrate, calcification, the tubercle bacilli gnawing at lung tissue. Caving formation - literal holes in the organ. Necrosis at the center. Perhaps the result of a single sneeze inhaled on the street somewhere. He remembered the red, swollen eyes, the pallor, the bloody phlegm, the lassitude of every patient. No wonder those free of the disease associated its victims with vampirism. Parrish began to work that afternoon, using varied shades of blue to achieve a three-dimensional effect—azure, cerulean, cobalt, periwinkle, royal, sapphire, ultramarine, indigo—cobalt to accentuate the depth of the cavings. No luminescence for these grotesqueries. Violent slashes of flat color, of blue, Deco ferocity, no mercy. No signature. Something new and abominable, the direction of modern art. This one would not be duplicated or mass produced.

Cline and Nurse Brady feigned enthusiasm, but the painting clearly eluded and disappointed them.

"I'll hang it in the bedroom, you know, like a trophy or something. Told you I'd whip the bastards."

"Hang it anywhere you want, but do me a favor. Don't tell anybody I painted it, ok? They'd never believe you anyway."

"Sure," said Cline, "how come?"

"It's not my style. I don't paint this sort of thing. It's renegade. I only did it for you, so I'd rather no one knew about it."

"Renegade, eh?" Cline liked the idea. "What's the other one?"

"Open it later."

"Ok—and mum's the word. Nobody comes here anyhow."

An uncomfortable silence engulfed the trio. They all seemed miserable and depressed.

After a few moments Parrish said, "Well, it does look a bit run down here. Have you thought about having somebody patch up the place? After all, it's a mansion."

"I hate it," groaned Nurse Brady. Cline nodded. If she hated it then he too hated it.

"You could move out. It's much too big for two people."

"Three. Who'd take care of *him*?" Cline said, pointing toward the ceiling. "Doc won't budge. And, you know, he saved both our lives... hey, and yours too. We can't just abandon him. He'd fall down the stairs or get electrocuted. He ain't the athlete he used to be."

Just then they heard the tapping of a cane in the hall and soon Dr. Tuth himself appeared in the doorway, wizened and jaundiced but spry enough. His eyes were gauzy translucent discs. Parrish had what he wanted. Titanium, a bit more titanium. He had put it in skies, trees, water, everything, but always too sparingly.

The old man raised his nose into the air and sniffed. "Somebody's here," he growled, laboring over to the table.

"It's me, Dr. Tuth, Maxfield Parrish. Do you remember me? I was your patient here a long time ago."

"Parrish! Of course I remember you, boy. The shy one. I hear you're famous."

"Well..."

"Not that I can see what you're famous for, mind you, but I remember some of those paintings. Did you ever finish the one you were doing out on the terrace?"

"Which one?"

"Come on, son, how am I supposed to know that? Seen one painting, seen them all. Trifles, after all."

He swallowed a mouthful of coffee, much of which leaked down his chin and onto the oilcloth draped over the table. Parrish and Nurse Brady exchanged glances.

"I guess you mean the *Century* covers... sure, I finished them."

"How are your lungs? Must be pretty good if you're still kicking. Got a lot of moribunds around here."

"He thinks we still have patients," Nurse Brady whispered to Parrish.

"My lungs are perfect, thanks to you," he lied.

"Son, I know you went to Arizona."

"Yes, but–"

"It's because you lacked faith. The Volt-O-Vap only cures those who believe in it. That's what's wrong these days, nobody believes. Parrish, I always thought the anarchists and unions would wreck this country. They didn't. You know what did? Our own government! Sheeet, man, the FDA hounded me out of business. Lot of dead folks would be walking around right now if they'd let me use my machine."

"I didn't know."

"Sure you didn't. It was all hushed up. Nobody, including me, wanted a scandal."

Cline slid his hand onto Dr. Tuth's shoulder. "Come on, Doc, you ought not to think about it. Don't want to get worked up, you know how lousy it makes you feel. Hey, eat some eggs."

"Don't want eggs," the old man replied petulantly, pushing the plate away.

"Parrish," he went on, "they tortured me. Sued me for every cent I had. Wanted to throw me in jail too, but I bought my way out."

"What could they possibly sue you over?" Parrish asked.

"False advertising and fraud, that's what they said. They finally got me on a Volt-O-Vap ad in some magazine around 1920, right after the war. Went all through the courts. By the time they finished I was ruined. Then these blasted cataracts, though they didn't blind me. Damned x-rays blinded me. If it wasn't for Cline and the nurse, sheeet, they'd have buried me."

Parrish glanced at Cline, who shrugged. "I saved up a little, you know, over the years. When I seen what they done down in Coral Gables I bought some lots—hey, I told you about Florida, remember? Anyway, I made enough off the deal to finish paying Doc's bills and keep us going here. We ain't got much left but, hell, we don't starve. We ain't hopping box cars."

"That means bananas," Dr. Tuth groaned.

"Told you he didn't like bananas."

Dr. Tuth shot up suddenly from his chair, cleared his throat and started banging on the table with the tip of his cane. "The Czar requests a song!" he proclaimed.

"Here it comes," said Cline, "no warning, you know."

Dr. Tuth proceeded to sing the refrain from "On the Banks of the Wabash" exactly as he had so often in the past. He didn't miss a word.

Parrish turned back to Cline, who winked and thumped his head with forefinger. Nurse Brady shuffled over in her slippers and started to lead the old man away.

"Nurse, give Parrish another dose of vapors. He doesn't look so good today," Dr. Tuth fussed as they left the room.

"He gets real daft sometimes," Cline explained. "Once in a while I pretend I'm the Czar, the one they killed. I tried to tell him they don't have czars no more, but he looks at me like I was an idiot and says, 'There will always be czars. Modesty is the virtue of peasants. God save the realm.' It gets pretty bad. She's going to put him to bed. That's where he spends most of his time, lying there like one of these here bananas."

He started to clear off the table and became preoccupied enough for Parrish to slip out onto to what was left of the terrace and make a few rough sketches of the lake. It looked far more agitated and redolent than he remembered, as if being subsumed by a slow-burning, subtle fire. A lake on fire! Surely his eyes deceived him. Rising gracefully over the foothills, the sun cast a golden silt-like haze across the entire valley. Anything could happen in such a place.

Much of the terrace had already toppled over the mountain. One column lay shattered on the slope, and the other looked as if it too would give way any moment. Allowing himself to be swept away on a wave of keen nostalgia, Parrish actually found himself missing the days where everyone lay dying in the redwood chairs and Nurse Brady sang her silly tunes and Dr. Tuth rushed about like some crazed Disney character. He now understood what Lydia had been after down at Bloody Marsh. The Negroes were her lake and valley, and she had immortalized them by recording what little they had, their folk tales; it was the only way to keep them from disappearing forever, as surely they would, as this building and mountain and valley, despite seeming durability, would surely disappear, as the stars would vanish from the heavens, as the laws of nature themselves would ultimately fail.

Nurse Brady suddenly appeared at Parrish's side. She'd hastily coiffured her hair and applied layers of makeup. She had unwrapped the other picture, which she carried under her arm.

"It's beautiful," she said, "but not me."

"If it was you once, it's still you," Parrish said, still gazing off into the valley, distraught by his lie.

"It doesn't look like the things you paint. No blue."

"You're right," he laughed, "a man named Gibson should have done it. He would have done a much better job. You must promise that no one will ever know I painted it - like the lung. We illustrators try not to step on each other's toes."

"Because it's not the kind of thing you do, I know."

He turned to find her gazing into his eyes, that look again, a haunting from the past, the past that forgets it has passed. He felt irritable, uneasy.

"Mr. Parrish–"

"It's impossible, not now, not then. I am the fool who missed the train. I read a novel once where somebody said, 'You can't repeat the past.'"

She seemed taken aback, insulted. Her face turned scarlet. "It's nothing like that."

Parrish apologized. How arrogant of him to think...

"I only want to tell you something, two things, before Cline gets back. He drove to the village for more bananas and coffee. I don't know if you'll want to hear what I have to say."

"But I should? Even after all this time?"

"Yes."

"Not three but four of us live here. Not long after you left here I had a child."

Parrish clutched a chunk of concrete balustrade for support. His heart pounded.

"He's twenty-nine years old, a man already, and will inherit this place, what's left of it. Dr. Tuth made a will."

Parrish stood overwhelmed and speechless.

"Cline is a perfect father. He loves his son. They fish together, hunt, gamble down at the tavern. Sometimes, anyway."

"But... 1901, was Cline capable? He was dying as I recall."

"Let's say he was capable."

Parrish pulled out a handkerchief and wiped his brow. Why had he vaguely expected news of this sort?

"Where is your son?"

"He's upstairs. I want you to meet him before

you leave."

"Yes, surely, I must meet him," Parrish mumbled.

"And something else. When Dr. Tuth mentioned the charges against him, he didn't exactly lie, but there's more to it. I don't think he remembers the worst. It was horrible."

"Other charges? Look, Nurse Brady, I'm not prepared–"

"Murder."

"Oh come on, woman! Murder? Dr. Tuth? I don't believe it."

"I said that was the charge. He didn't murder anybody, of course, but when the FDA started that business with the Volt-O-Vap, they also came round to take a look at his x-ray machine. You recall how he waited for it, month after month after month. In those days nobody knew much about how dangerous they were. Dr. Tuth used to expose his patients, the ones who were going to die anyway, to ungodly dosages. He thought it might incinerate the tubercles. Short potent doses three or four times a day. The father of one of these patients, whose burned skin turned gangrenous, talked to a lawyer who convinced him that Dr. Tuth was liable. And that's it... except for the trial, which was indecent if you ask me. They carried the patient in on a stretcher. He was dying of cancer."

"Was Dr. Tuth convicted?"

"Yes, but not of homicide. They called it negligent manslaughter or something like that. The judge didn't sentence him because of his reputation. He had to pay a fine and make restitution to the patient, who died two weeks later. He was placed under house arrest more or less, but no one ever came round to check."

"It's so unfair. All Dr. Tuth ever wanted was to

cure people."

"It unhinged his mind. He couldn't concentrate on much after that ordeal. And you see how he is now, though now age is the culprit."

Parrish peered down over the hillside cluttered with scrub brush and pieces of the House of Invalids. "I see how everyone is now."

Nurse Brady hooked the bend of his arm. "Come, I want you to see my son."

She led him up the stairs to an isolated door at the end of a dim, chilly vestibule, knocked gently and without waiting for a reply entered the room. Parrish followed her apprehensively, as he had so often in the past. Someone slouched in a stuffed armchair beside the window. When Nurse Brady pulled the chain of an old brass standing lamp the room became a yellow bubble, and the occupant of the chair covered both eyes with his hands.

"Charles!" Said Nurse Brady sternly, "someone's come to visit you. Wouldn't you like to say hello?"

Charles turned slowly at his mother's command, but the presence of a stranger frightened him and he refused to budge from the chair. Parrish had seen enough. The young man's gauzy, translucent skin draped over his bones like fine silk. The cropped red hair and lack of eyebrows intensified his pallor. Parrish assumed he was the victim of some ghastly disease that had undermined not only his constitution but his mental capacity as well. His speech and movements were awkward and ill-timed. He made gurgling sounds as Nurse Brady bent over to kiss him. One of his eyes looked moist and swollen and was ringed with bruise-like discoloration. His lower lip sagged like Woodrow Wilson's after the stroke.

"One of his bad days," Nurse Brady sighed to

Parrish. Then, turning to her son, "Charles, I want you to meet Mr. Parrish, the famous painter."

Something tortured came of out Charles' mouth as he extended a limp, veiny hand. The gesture seemed wholly contrived as if it were some ritual he had been forced to learn along the way without having the slightest idea of what it signified. Parrish grasped the hand and felt it turn to mush.

"Are you shocked?" asked Nurse Brady.

"Well–"

"Don't worry, he won't understand."

"What's wrong with him? I've never seen–"

"He had tuberculosis."

"And it did *this*?"

"No, I guess not. I don't know. Maybe the x-ray treatments. Who knows how these things happen?"

"It must be very hard for you," Parrish groaned, aching for something to do with his hands.

"Not really, I'm just thankful he didn't die. The x-rays did cure his lungs, you know."

"The x-rays."

"Yes, thanks to Dr. Tuth. That's something anyway. And this really is one of his bad, bad days. He does get up and around. Usually he's quite the worker. He goes into town for supplies sometimes, he sweeps, gardens... and he's very good with Dr. Tuth. They're great buddies. Dr. Tuth has taught him to sing. It's hard to believe but Charles has a beautiful voice."

"What about his mind?" Parrish asked, regretting the question instantly.

"I never know what he's thinking or if he's thinking at all. Nobody does. He may be a genius. Who can tell?"

Suddenly there issued from Charles' mouth a forlorn cry of unspeakable agony, a sound Parrish had never heard before in his life—like hundreds of birds careening into a sheet of glass.

"The light hurts his eyes," Nurse Brady said hurriedly. We'd better go." She twirled her key ring and walked out the door.

"Goodbye, Charles, I'm glad we've met," said Parrish, taking his final glance back at him.

Charles bobbed his head, grinned and stuck out his tongue. Parrish, in his haste to leave, nearly stumbled over the transom. He was terrified.

She trailed behind as he headed for the car and began to toss his luggage onto the back seat. A single thought repeated itself: this woman IS yearning, not a woman yearning, she IS yearning, yearning itself.

"Why don't you wait for Cline at least? You know he thinks the world of you. He wanted to write to you about Florida."

"Why didn't he?" Parrish tried to laugh.

"He said it would embarrass you. He thinks you're too sensitive."

"I'm the one who's embarrassed," he said, tossing, finally, the valise atop the rest of the luggage. "I really believe I should go. And he's right about the 'sensitive.'"

"Not because of Charles?"

"What do you think?"

"I think you shouldn't worry about it. Cline is his father. Cline loves Charles. You should stay a while. We have history."

"It's not that," Parrish said, "I don't know how to explain... it's me, I suppose... I get this feeling that time moves backwards here and I'm not sure I like it, not yet. I think you should get out of here too, all of you. This place is a ruin. Has too many ghosts. Maybe memories are the ghosts."

He slid into the driver's seat and started the ignition. "Maybe I could send you a check, you know, every now and then... to help out. I would like to help–"

"We have all we need," Nurse Brady said abruptly.

He studied her for a moment, the porcelain face now metamorphosed into sturdy old, splotched marble, her once dreamy eyes riveted on him with both anger and frustration, the moist puffy lips of yesteryear faded and cracked. Time is relative all right. She was a survivor, though, as always, however cruel the bludgeons of time. He thought about senile Dr. Tuth and monstrous Charles, about Cline and his silly bananas, about their fragile lungs, how it was their lungs that had brought them together and made them inseparable no matter how far apart they might drift. He saw that is was better to be young and dying than old and healthy, for old age meant suffering the losses of a never-ending past. The future shrank, the past evolved. He remembered youth as a time when anything was possible, when one could align one's prospects with each never day and recreate the world— even as one lay dying of tuberculosis on the terrace of a splendid mansion in one of earth's paradises.

"That's what my paintings are all about!" he cried in surprise.

"What?" she asked.

"Nothing," he said, floored the accelerator and drove away. Adams' Dynamo was time. Time is sorrow.

IV.

The old man watched from a shattered window inside one of the long, drafty halls. Charles Cline, now haggard and well over sixty years old, played a game with himself, a child's game of flinging playing cards against the wall. He had grown ludicrously fat in his old age. He sat atop a mound of rubble and broken glass on what was left of the terrace and, turning from the cards, methodically disassembled a daisy. "My mommy," Charles chanted as he plucked one of the petals, "my daddy," tossing aside another, "my mommy, my daddy, my mommy, my daddy, my mommy..."

He had no reason to suspect he was not alone. He had been alone for a long time, ever since he dug the holes in the cellar. Aside from occasional intruders who departed quickly enough once they beheld Charles brandishing a battered Yankee Slugger, no one ever visited the final lord and master of The House of Invalids. He had dug the first hole nearly twenty years ago when he found Cline slumped over a stack of firewood, the ax by his side. Charles had never seen a dead person and refused at first to be consoled. He demanded of Nurse Brady that she explain to him repeatedly that Cline's heart was so sick that it made him go away. She told him that when people died other people hid them in the ground. She said they would do that for Daddy and that he, Charles, would have to dig because she lacked the strength. Upset and frightened, Charles obeyed his mother, and together they dragged the swollen, inert body down some rickety stairs. He dug a massive hole in the gloomy, dark cellar—not far from the remnants of Dr. Tuth's x-ray machine.

A few years later it was Nurse Brady's time to go away, and dutiful Charles dug another hole beside Cline's. He did not think to erect markers on the graves, and only recently dreamed that his mother had come out of the cellar and told him to dig a third hole for himself, for when *he* went away. This he did, only dimly aware that there was no one left to hide him in it, no one but Blinky upstairs, and Blinky never moved. Charles thought Blinky should have gone away a long time ago. Blinky scared him. Maybe he should *make* Blinky go away. Sometimes he carried Blinky around in a basket. Blinky was a hazy eyeball now embedded in a gel of protoplasm.

Had Charles known he was being observed, he would have run away to hide in one of the wonderful secret places he'd discovered over the years, the dusty crypts concealed behind false bookcases, the empty armoires and closets, trap doors leading to underground tunnels and stacks of mildewed boxes in Blinky's old office, some of which could hold a man. But the observer concealed his presence. He had no idea how Charles would react to a stranger, for he surely would not have remembered him, and he felt no desire for another encounter. He could not forget Charles' sagging purple tongue and had not reappeared to come to terms with it. He wanted to speak with Nurse Brady. He had prowled the building in search of her, found no evidence of her presence and feared the worst. After all, it had been thirty-three years. The intruder had nothing at all to say to Charles. Was Charles his son?

Parrish sensed that the closer one drew nigh to the present, the more personal time became. His early years, the story of American progress, could be represented in the past tense, third person, that is, the historical sense. To approach the present meant losing history and immersing oneself in the immediate flux— the minute human exchanges, the daily vicissitudes of gains and losses, the eye blinks and sighs and yawns and belches and the entire array of human effusions and ejaculations that get swept away by historical chronicles of any era. Did Napoleon ever yawn? The question is irrelevant, absurd.

December 31, 1965: *I scratch these last words with great difficulty. My fingers, gnarled and brittle as twigs, do not manage a pencil well. I can no longer paint. It is my bones, not my lungs, that betray me... no, nothing has betrayed me except time, the usual culprit.*

Why I write these notes to myself I cannot say. My housekeeper will burn them, as instructed, and I pray she has burned the rest of them. How can I, who know the syntax and resonance of color, trust mere words? Even deaf mutes understand color. It belongs to and reflects nature, unlike words, which reflect only themselves and therefore have no meaning. Saboteurs. Yet what I paint, or used to paint, is not true to the world either. Art goes beyond what it reflects, there's the secret, and my only obligation to the world would have been to die even prior to my arrival at The House of Invalids. In the nineteenth century! It is a supreme aberration that I should have been chosen, if chosen is the word, to linger on into the twentieth - and so deeply into it! Art freed me of disease, so to speak, enabled me to create my own private sanctuary out of what has proved the most vile, evil era in history. And I have paid the price for that privilege.

That my life has been long, prosperous and happy is true enough. I've never lacked the small luxuries most men spend a lifetime failing to obtain. Yet what do these luxuries finally signify? An easier time at the bank, a new wardrobe or car... so what? Luxury has nothing to do with truth, and I have lived far too long to escape my share of truth. I admire the young writer in California who says he enjoys the taste of hot dogs cooked over an open fire and doused with yellow mustard. I know the feeling. It's like a simple daybreak rushing into your soul, terrifying in its simplicity. If simplicity does not terrify then why have we gone to such lengths to complicate it? All this talk about atom bombs and nuclear fission—who can begin to fathom the enormity? I was born before the discovery of the atom! And now men routinely split it apart. What next? I always ask myself, what next? I have never ceased to underestimate mankind. Or is it that I overestimate?

The sole advantage of old age is perspective, and yet the old cannot implement that perspective to any advantage. You cannot teach this to a young man, for in his zeal to triumph over endless trifles he forgets that he himself will age. When the president was assassinated two years ago the nation grieved, which is only proper, but they do not remember the others as I do. I was there, the same shenanigans repeated over and over again without television. But this president was special, they say, forgetting that I have seen two Roosevelt's and Wilson in office. What was so special? His youth? Good looks? His beautiful wife? Nurse Brady in her day was far more beautiful. And so was Lydia, bless her gentle, patient soul. When I think of her and of my madness, my work, always coming first, at the expense of our marriage, I want to rise out of this wheelchair and force back the clock until time chokes on itself. What is fame? Obscurity? Say I had been a poor man, a common worker... would I not have gone to my grave at some decent age, content with the knowledge that I had been true to my nature, it to me? Who is Parrish? Hs is his pictures, and Outcast Unknown, the man who stepped out of reality and time and into a vision.

How I crave the reality now that time has run out. Not to paint the day breaking but to receive it directly, without mediation, not as an observer who feels the need to possess or change it. Even tuberculosis could not deter me. Perhaps I survived despite rather than because of my art. Perhaps I am not an artist after all. The profundity of art lies in its refusal to compromise: it kills. The list of martyrs is long and legendary and needs no enumeration here. My name will not be found among them. I do not have a reputation for profundity.

No illustrator does. Because people do not buy what they cannot understand; it disturbs them if it registers at all. So in order to survive the illustrator prostitutes himself and draws pictures of underwear or perfume bottles or candy boxes, whatever the people want. Every illustrator worth his salt works on a periphery where art and reality meet, but he distorts reality, unlike the artist who sees truth behind and within reality and depicts that truth. Not more money, glory, although they may follow. The artist remains a poor man, whatever his net worth, and lives like one. This I have not done or fear I have not done. Had my painting failed to support me would I have abandoned it? The question haunts me. A man at ease with himself, a Cline for instance, asks himself no such questions. He purchases lots in Coral Gables and settles down with a ravaged Gibson Girl.

And yet, ah, it was an illustrator who created her for Cline. Charles Dana Gibson. I knew him and once succumbed to his dream myself. Imagine. Being lured into another artist's dream! Who am I to judge myself? Or Nurse Brady? Or anyone?

He did not like the lung I painted for him because it was blue. But I could hardly paint it any other color since that's the way it came to me. Even

I, a cartoon character with dollar signs in my eyes, must rely upon what comes. I should have waited for him. Nurse Brady knew it all the time; it was Charles. I could not admit the fact of Charles. I have devoted my life to achieving the only kind of perfection I know, and Charles represented the abomination that belied it all. I wanted to create a perfect, timeless romance... a lie, that is. I did not know truth always lurks on the borders of romance, that it could take the form of a Charles. Charles. Caliban. Inheritor.

The impatient young man took one look at his ancient, feeble passenger and became fussy and disconsolate, until, that is, the old man gave him a roll of cash and promised more. "We will stop near Burlington for the night," he coughed, "I can no longer tolerate long journeys." Long? The driver sighed deeply. He had to lift the specimen out of his wheelchair and practically toss him into the back seat. He weighed no more than a feather. The chair and canes went into the trunk. Soyez, or whatever his name, began to chat nervously as soon as they had climbed the entrance ramp onto an expressway. He tuned on the radio, which he knew would irritate his passenger. One thing old people cannot stand is noise, even good noise. A subtle form of sabotage, but effective. Who in the fuck wants to be old? He gazed into the rearview at the living corpse he was taking God know where. The end of the line probably, he chuckled to himself as the Beatles' "I Want to Hold Your Hand" ricocheted all over the walls of the taxi. The young man yawned and belched at once.

"What kind of work you in, Pops?" he asked

"Painting," Parrish grunted.

"Hey, neat... I used to paint before I got my

cab here. Did lots of houses in Manchester. Don't like these new latexes much. Oil, man, there's your real paint."

As they approached Burlington Parrish noticed a sprawling outdoor flea market set back in the woods off the service road. He instructed the driver to pull in so he could take a look around. DEALERS FROM TEN STATES proclaimed a massive sign dotted with yellow light bulbs that didn't work. The Dealers from Ten States had arranged their wares on an endless chain of cafeteria-style tables set up directly on the grass, and crowds of people busily inspected everything from used shoes to sets of lug wrenches. Parrish emerged from the cab only with Soyez's help. It seemed an unusually bad day although he could still walk, or rather hobble, by balancing himself on the two canes and taking slow, deliberated, calculated steps every moment or so. The pace drove Soyez out of his mind.

"Pops," he growled, "let me get your wheels out of the trunk. Wait here, you going to fall down, man. Can't be too careful when you old. Man, hope I never get old."

Parrish glanced back wearily, sympathized. "Yes," he said, "the chair."

Soyez pushed Parrish up three or four aisles before the old man signaled him to stop at a display of old magazine ads and books and prints. The man behind the counter did not bother to rise from his lawn chair; he was sliding baseball cards into small plastic bags and looked intently preoccupied. He had purple lips, Parrish observed. A sign taped onto the edge of the table read: MR NOSTLAGIA.

"Need help?" asked Mr. Nostalgia, not bothering to lift his droopy, wide eyes. "I got the Honus Wagner baseball card. Give it to you cheap."

Parrish's voice was frail and distant, always frail and distant now, for he could no longer speak above a whisper. No one takes a man seriously who cannot raise his voice, he'd discovered. Or move faster than a tortoise.

"How much is that picture over there?" he asked, pointing one of his canes at a small, bluish scene in a battered frame. He could not see it clearly, could no longer see anything except through a gauze-like miasma, but thought it might be "Dinky Bird."

"That one?" the man finally looked up. "That's a Parrish. They're starting to go high now. Let you have it for seventy-five bucks if it's cash. Try buying it in the city—three, four hundred bucks."

Only seventy-five? Well, a mediocre print after all, one of thousands like it.

"What's Parrish?" asked Parrish.

Mr. Nostalgia had begun to undo the frame from its hook on a portable pegboard wall. "Maxwell Parrish," he said. "He painted lots of blue stuff like this back in the twenties. Real collectible now. Manhattan this would go for a mint, but we ain't in Manhattan, are we? That's why I'm letting you have it for seventy-five. That's the original House of Art frame too."

He held the picture at arm's length so Parrish could look it over.

"Don't see much in it myself. The women, though, they go crazy for Parrish. This is a famous one, 'Daybreak' or something like that. I don't know, maybe it's called 'Sunrise.' All look the same to me. The frame's gotta be blue and gold."

"This Parrish... is he still alive?"

Mr Nostalgic shrugged, cleared his throat. "I don't know, probably dead by now. He'd be pretty old.

I'd say he was probably dead but don't quote me."

Probably dead. Better dead? As rendered by a man with purple lips and a fondness for baseball cards.

"Anything by Normal Rockwell?"

"Rockwell? He's hotter than Parrish and still alive. I can sell Rockwell's in a flash, not the originals, I never get those, collectors and museums grabbing them all up. You're talking money there. *Saturday Evening Post* covers—I just sold one he did of Kennedy for a hundred. Got a little less for Ike, but what can you expect? They should have shot Ike too. I've got tons of Ike stuff. Minute somebody dies, up goes the price. Let's see... Rockwell... the first *Post* cover he did, that's choice. You're close to a grand there. You interested? I know a guy who's got one, give it to you for five hundred. Now that is a good deal."

Parrish felt queasy and wanted to return to the cab.

"No," he said, "just give me the *Maxwell* Parrish. He pulled ten ten-dollar bills out of the valise he had wedged between his hip and the wheelchair arm and passed the bills to Mr. Nostalgia, a transaction that did not escape Soyez's hungry eyes, which, Parrish had noted earlier, were black.

"You collect Parrish?" Mr. Nostalgia asked as he wrapped the print in newspaper. "That's good, not my style, though, too blue, know what I mean? The world ain't blue. Never seen so much blue."

He gave the print to Soyez to carry.

"Not blue," said Parrish. "Cobalt, verdigris, ultramarine... not mere blue."

Mr. Nostlagia's purple lips parted in self-defense at the challenge.

"Not blue, eh? Whatever you say, here's your

change, you gave me too much. Call it what you want, blue is blue, and that's blue, old-timer. You know who goes crazy over it besides women? Pansies. They love it. A pansy can't live without Parrishes."

His words were wasted on Parrish for Soyez had already wheeled him away.

Blue.

Suppose I were required to eliminate one color from the spectrum, from the universe... which would I choose? Oddly, I believe it would be blue. It hardly seems real to me. Sometimes I think I invented it. I can't imagine a world without its reds and greens and yellows, even its blacks, but a blueless world, I can. The women love it. They say atoms have no color."

It is no coincidence that Negroes call their music the blues. Or that the word rhymes with rue.

I have even heard of blue people. And of course, the sky.

Charles was blue, a shade I've never seen before, and I have seen every shade. The difference between my blues and those of Charles is life itself. Not health, I said life, the little of it Charles had left in him. I could never mix such a color. Is Charles my son? I finally had to know, which is why I returned once again to the House of Invalids what now seems so many years ago, long after Cline and Nurse Brady were no more. Not a casual undertaking for an aging, decrepit man. Journeys can kill people my age, even my age then, but so can anything, a quick twist of the neck, a draft, a thunderclap, the thought of a girl. Borrowed time, yes, but borrowed from whom? I have lived without a future for so long I've forgotten what future feels like. A long time ago I stepped into my "Daybreak" and have not yet fully emerged.

I had no idea at the time that my old friends had passed. It's difficult to remember now what I intended... I supposed I planned to put the question directly to Nurse Brady. When it became apparent that no one was around except creepy Charles, whose footsteps resounded on an upper floor, I sneaked into Dr. Tuth's old office where thousands of hand-written records had been filed in countless wooden cabinets. I really couldn't say what I expected to find, certainly not a birth certificate. After an hour or so of thumbing through files I came upon my own admission records of so long ago. And my discharge as well. These did not interest me. I wanted specifics on Charles. After what seemed a long while I grew impatient and weary and realized no such records would exist. A kind of relief. No more dwelling upon what in fact had little import. Nurse Brady had insisted that Cline was the father. Let it go at that. Yet you can always tell when a woman subterfuges. They get that look. They draw the curtain. They make it obvious what is obvious then turn it around. Let it go. Cline is the father.

What I did not expect to find was my portrait of the art deco lung stuffed behind one of the file cabinets. It had gathered dust and greasy spider webs. Someone had punctured a fist-sized hole right through the canvass. No doubt Cline. He feared the picture, hated it. Why I do not know unless it represented to him everything that was wrong with the world. Or maybe he found is simply ugly. I am not proud of the work myself although it was an original, a one-of-a-kind, not mass produced like all the others. And remember I write this from memory; this happened some years ago and I can no longer remember details. I am presently in a noisy cab driven by an insolent driver on my way home for good.

And what if I had come upon Charles? I would have fled. He could not have remembered me. And thus Charles had become for me what the blue lung signified for Cline: a refusal to accept what has been given.

I stepped into my luminosities; Cline into his domesticity with bananas and alcohol. We were more alike than I could ever have imagined. And perhaps this is the way with all of us — outright denial, erecting mythologies of bedazzlement to blind us from preposterous realities.

In the end this can be said: I came into this world, I grew ill, I attempted to change my station, I was cured, I failed to change anything (because history out-paced me), I aged, and now... there is a filthy painting of a blue art deco lung in a mansion about to collapse and that painting has a jagged hole in it. And you can still find my prints at flea markets all over the country even as our country explodes with chaos and protest and disenchantment. Who will paint these times? Who will paint the way out?

Shortly, I shall return to the past.

Three volumes of Louis Gallo's poetry, *Archaeology*, *Scherzo Furiant* and *Clearing the Attic*, are now available. Three forthcoming volumes, *Crash, Why is there Something Rather than Nothing?* and *Leeway & Advent*, will be published in the near future. His work will appear in Best Short Fiction 2020 forthcoming.

Thank you to the Wapshott Press sponsors, supporters, and Friends of the Wapshott Press.

Muna Deriane
Kit Ramage
Rachel Livingston
Laurel Sutton
Thomas Loper
Kathleen Warner
Ann and John Brantingham
David Meischen
John O'Kane
Suzanne Siegel
Toni Rodriguez
LindaAnn LoSchiavo
James and Rebecca White
Robert Earle and Mary Azoy
Steve Misuraca
Alice Frances Wickham
James Wilson
Phil Temples
Richard Whittaker
Ann Siemens
Kathy Bonagofsky

The Wapshott Press is a 501(c)(3) not-for-profit press publishing work by emerging and established authors and artists. We publish books that should be published. We are very grateful to the people who believe in our plans and goals, as well as our hopes and dreams. Our website is at www.WapshottPress.org. Donations gratefully accepted at www.Donate.WapshottPress.org.